Alaska

Double Trouble Series

Daina Sargent has lived in several states but considers Arkansas her home. Born in California and raised in Arkansas, she graduated from West Fork High School with honors, in 1981. Daina attended college in Jonesboro, Arkansas and Tulsa, Oklahoma. She plans to continue her education. Daina has three daughters.

Alaska

Double Trouble Series

By Daina Sargent

Illustrated by Jane Lenoir

Ozark Publishing, Inc.
P.O. Box 228
Prairie Grove, AR 72753

Cataloging-in-Publication Data

Sargent, Daina, 1963–
    Alaska / by Daina Sargent ; illustrated by
Jane Lenoir. —Prairie Grove, AR : Ozark
Publishing, c2005.
      p. cm. (Double trouble series)
      "Be brave"—Cover.
      SUMMARY: While Liz is reading a book
about Alaska to her twin brother, Matt, a large
oval mirror in the room begins glowing and
twinkling. It goes crazy, shooting rainbows
of light everywhere. Suddenly, they hear a loud
Whoosh and realize that they are being
transported somewhere. They land with a
big thud in a snowbank.
      ISBN 1-59381-120-9 (hc)
             1-59381-121-7 (pbk)
      1. Alaska—Juvenile fiction. 2. Dogsledding—
Juvenile fiction. 3. Eskimos—Juvenile fiction.
4. Iditarod trail sled dog race, Alaska—Juvenile
fiction. [1. Alaska—Fiction. 2. Dogsledding—
Fiction. 3. Eskimos—Fiction] I. Sargent, Daina,
1963– II. Jane Lenoir, 1950– ill. III. Title.
IV. Series.
      PZ7.S24Al 2005
      [Fic]—dc21   2003099973

Printed in the United States of America

Inspired by

My main inspiration for all of my books has to be my daddy. He is the one who encouraged me and asked me to use my imagination. For Alaska, I like snow!

Dedicated to

I would like to dedicate my first book to several people who brought me to this point.

The first dedication goes to my daughters, Amber, April and Ashley. Thank you for being such great daughters and turning out to be my friends. I love you.

The next dedication goes to my dad, Dave Sargent. It is because of you that I even tried this. You have always been a positive influence in my life. I love you.

To the people listed above, you are the best team anyone could ask for. I thank all of you very much for listening to my stories over and over. We finally made it to print!

Foreword

While Liz is reading a book about Alaska to her twin brother, Matt, a large oval mirror in the room begins glowing and twinkling. It goes crazy, shooting rainbows of light everywhere. Suddenly, they hear a loud Whoosh and realize that they are being transported somewhere. They land with a big thud in a snowbank.

Contents

Alaska

Double Trouble Series

If you would like to have the author of the Double Trouble Series visit your school, free of charge, call 1-800-321-5671.

One

The Magic Mirror

One spring day, early in the morning, Matthew Frederick and Elizabeth Natasha were born. They were the first set of twins to be born in the family. Matthew became Matt and Elizabeth, Liz. They were real characters with vivid imaginations and wonderful personalities.

As they got older, the twins looked very different from each other. Matt grew an unruly head of flaming red hair. He had green eyes and freckles. He was tall and lanky. Liz had very blonde curly hair, piercing blue eyes, dimples and was short. She had to take two steps to Matt's one to keep up with him and looked like she was running. They had a bond and were best friends.

When the twins were born, they received a gift from a great aunt who lived in the Philippines.

Liz and Matt's mama opened it. It was an astoundingly beautiful oval wall mirror, trimmed in gold, silver and rhinestones.

Little did Matt and Liz know that this mirror was going to take them on many adventures.

Matt was an adventurer. He loved to use his imagination to go places. All he had to do was close his eyes and let his mind wander to take him away.

Liz was more studious. She always thought that the way Matt traveled was neat, but it was in her nature to read about the places. Together, they developed a way to go. Liz would read about the places, and Matt would close his eyes. When Liz was through reading, Matt would describe everything in detail.

One day, the twins decided to start traveling to every state in the United States and learn something about each one. They went to the library in their home. There Matt would lie down and put his head back on the floor with his hands

clasped behind it, imaging the different places as Liz read aloud.

Today, Liz was reading about Alaska. She started off by telling Matt the usual things like the state capital is Juneau. But there was an amusing thing about the capital. It can only be reached by boat or plane. The twins chuckled at this information. They were used to going everywhere in a car. Matt heard Liz say, "Wow, the state of Rhode Island could fit into Alaska 425 times. That must mean that Alaska is big!"

Suddenly, the mirror that hung on the wall of the library started to twinkle. Liz kept reading but from the corner of her eye, she could tell that something was happening. The mirror brightened and went crazy with sparks of color. It looked like the Fourth of July. The rhinestones started throwing rainbows of light everywhere.

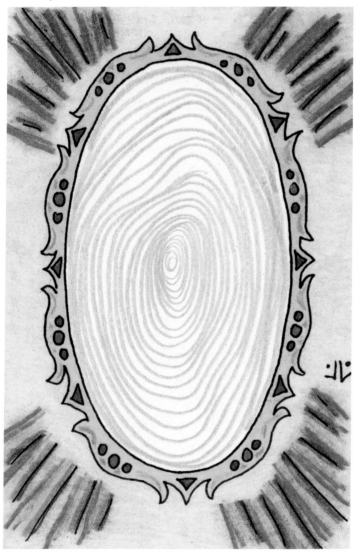

The children realized that they were being taken somewhere.

"Hold my hand," Matt shouted.

Liz grabbed Matt's hand and squeezed. "Where are we going? What's happening?" she asked. She was always so inquisitive.

"I don't know. Just hold on!" Matt exclaimed.

With a thud they landed in a bank of snow. Everywhere they looked it was white.

"Where are we and why are we dressed the way we are?" Liz asked.

"I don't know. Let's see if we can find someone to help us," said Matt. He too noticed that they were dressed differently than they had been when they were sitting in the library at home. There they had worn shorts, t-shirts, and sandals. Now they were dressed in layers of clothing, parkas, mittens, and boots. They each had a scarf, earmuffs, and a stocking cap.

Two

Alaska

WHOOSH!

The sound and the breeze that went by them were so loud and strong that it almost knocked them down.

Again Liz was full of questions. "Matt, what was that sound and what was that thing that went by us?"

Matt told Liz, "I don't know." Then there was another loud

WHOOSH!

These sounds were so unusual! But one sound they recognized—the whimpering of several dogs.

Liz and Matt identified the dogs as snow dogs. Attached to the dogs was a sled. The sled seemed rather small, but the twins weren't that big. They could both fit on it.

Obviously the Huskies had been left there for a reason. Perhaps it was part of the magic that had brought them to Alaska. There was no driver for the sled, and they did need transportation other than their feet. So Matt climbed on the sled and clutched the reins of the team that was harnessed together.

He said, "Get on, Liz."

Liz looked at Matt for a minute and then climbed on.

Matt yelled, "Go!"

The team didn't move.

Matt thought to himself, "What do I do to make the dogs go?"

Someone yelled, "Hey Kid, yell 'Let's go' or 'All right' and the team will take off!"

Matt did as he was told and the team took off like lightning.

Liz thought, "I've read all about mushing sleds and snow dogs. But did I tell Matt?" She was thinking about everything she had told Matt about Alaska, and she remembered telling him about dog mushing being a sled race with dogs.

"Liz, I think we may be in some race. I'm going to follow the trail the other sleds have made and maybe we can find someone who will help us get back home."

They soared in the sled. They traveled for an hour before they saw a group of sleds and dogs. The dogs were tied to their trucks, resting and drinking water. The twins stopped. They had cookies, beef jerky, and water with the sled drivers. It wasn't much of a dinner, but they had something in their stomachs now.

Matt wanted details about where they were and exactly what was happening. He waltzed up to one of the older men, an Eskimo.

"Excuse me, Sir," Matt said. "Could you please tell me where we are and what's going on?"

"You're in a dog race, Young Man," the Eskimo responded. "It's called the Iditarod."

What exactly is the Iditarod?" Matt questioned.

"It's the most well-known sled race in Alaska. We are now at the Cripple checkpoint. You'd better get all the water you can for you and the dogs, Son. Because there's not another checkpoint until Ruby."

The Eskimo looked down, then looked back at Matt with a surprised look on his face. "Wait a minute. You mean you have a sled and a team of dogs, and you don't know where you are or what's going on?"

Matt shrugged. "No Sir, I don't. My sister was reading a book to me about Alaska and we ended up here. I don't know how we got here

or how to get home. We'd appreci-
ate it if we could stay with you. We
have no food or water for the dogs,
or us." Matt was really frustrated.

"Son, are you sure you're ready for the next leg of the trip? The Iditarod is full of dangers. There are twists and turns, steep banks and icy hills. I'll be happy to help you but you have to stay right with me. Ruby is the next stop. When we get there, you'll need to scratch the race. We'll see if we can find you a way home." The Eskimo was offering help.

"What is scratching? I don't have an itch!" Matt was being funny.

"Scratching is when you drop out of the race from exhaustion, hurt, or your team isn't running right," the Eskimo explained.

Matt let Liz know what he had found out. They didn't have a choice except to wait for the rest of the teams and drivers. They were so tired. Liz could barely keep her eyes open, so she took a nap. Since they didn't really know anyone or where they were, Matt stayed awake.

Three

The Yukon River

Liz had been asleep for quite a while when she heard a commotion. She wished she knew how they had gotten here. "Maybe," she thought, "the oval mirror that Great Aunt Rita sent to us has something to do with us being here. Is that possible?" She would think about it today while they were mushing.

"Okay, Kids. It's time to go!" the Eskimo shouted.

"Do we have to go with them? I want to go home," Liz whined.

"This is the only way I know to get home, Liz. We're only going to the next stop. Why don't you look for wildlife, like elk or moose? Or look up. You could see an eagle." Matt was trying to cheer Liz up.

The twins climbed on the sled and Matt grabbed the reins. The lead dogs, Peter and Elliott, were ready. Their team was set to go. Matt pulled in behind the Eskimo and hollered, "Let's go!" to his team.

At times, it was dangerous. The Yukon River, which was usually frozen, was coming up.

Everyone in front of Matt and Liz made it across the river safely. Matt drove onto the icy river. There was a sudden loud cracking noise. The ice cracked and the team was disconnected from the sled.

The Eskimo looked back. He
stopped his team and ran to the river.

23

Everyone watched as the sled's rudders entered the water and went under the ice. The kids were gone.

The cracking ice was so loud to Matt and Liz! They were surprised. The boredom Liz had felt was gone. Matt was fearful for their lives! He had no reins or dog team. They knew they had fallen into the river. They saw the water. They were cold, but they were not wet. What was happening? This was a strange day. First, they had gone to Alaska, not knowing how. And now they were going somewhere else.

With a loud burst that sounded like a clap of thunder, the twins were unexpectedly back in their library.

They looked at themselves in the mirror. They no longer had on heavy winter clothing. They were dressed exactly like they were before they had gone to Alaska. The mirror was glistening with a faint glow.

"You okay, Liz?" Matt asked.

"Yeah," she answered. "Do you understand what just happened?"

"I'm not sure," Matt said. He walked up close to the mirror and pressed his face against it.

"Before we landed in the snow-bank in Alaska and raced in the Iditarod, you were reading about Alaska. Do you think this mirror is magic, Liz?"

"Some of the lights are still twinkling. I think it is magic!" Liz said.

Matt looked at the mirror and they decided that if the mirror was indeed magic, they couldn't wait to read about other states. What fun!

Four

Alaska Facts

Map of Alaska

State Flag

State Bird: Willow Ptarmigan

State Flower: Forget me Not

State Tree: Sitka Spruce

Agriculture: Seafood, nursery stock, dairy products, vegetables, and livestock

Did you know that oil is Alaska's most valuable natural resource? Alaska has an area that is thought to be North America's largest oil field. Alaska accounts for 25% of the oil produced in the US.

Something unique: Dog mushing is the official state sport.